GIFT

jE   Waddell, Martin
WAD   Sailor Bear.

For George
M.W.

For Samuel
V.A.

Text copyright © 1992 by Martin Waddell
Illustrations copyright © 1992 by Virginia Austin

First U.S. edition 1992
First published in Great Britain in 1992
by Walker Books Ltd., London.

Library of Congress Catalog Card Number 91-71822
Library of Congress Cataloging-in-Publication Data.

Waddell, Martin.
Sailor Bear / by Martin Waddell : illustrated by Virginia Austin.
—1st U.S. ed.
"First published in Great Britain in 1992 by Walker Books Ltd.,
London"—T.p. verso.
Summary : Lost and lonely, a little bear embarks on a rather
perilous sailing venture, but winds up with his heart's desires realized.
ISBN 1-56402-040-1
[1. Bears—Fiction. 2. Sailing—Fiction.] I. Austin, Virginia, 1951-
II. Title.
PZ7.W1137Sai   1992
[E]—dc20   91-71822

10 9 8 7 6 5 4 3 2

Printed and bound in Hong Kong.

The right of Martin Waddell to be identified
as author of this work has been asserted by him in
accordance with the Copyright, Designs, and Patents Act 1988.

Candlewick Press
2067 Massachusetts Avenue
Cambridge, Massachusetts 02140

Sailor Bear

by
Martin Waddell

illustrated by
Virginia Austin

CANDLEWICK PRESS
CAMBRIDGE, MASSACHUSETTS

Small Bear was a bear
in a sailor suit
who was lost
and had no one to play with.
"Now what shall I do?"
wondered Small Bear.

He thought and he thought.
Then he looked at his suit,
and he *knew* what to do.

"I'll be a sailor and sail on the sea!"
decided Small Bear.
But he didn't have a boat.
"Now what shall I do?"
wondered Small Bear.

He thought and he thought.
Then he looked at the sea,
and he *knew* what to do.

"I'll go and get one!"
decided Small Bear.
He went to the harbor,
but the boats there
were too big for a bear.
"Now what shall I do?"
wondered Small Bear.

He thought and he thought.
Then he looked around the shore,
and he *knew* what to do.

"Small bears need small boats,
so I'll make one!"
decided Small Bear.
He made a boat
from some pieces of wood
and half a barrel.
He called it "Bear's Boat,"
and he took it down to the sea.
BUT…

the sea looked too big for his boat.
"Now what shall I do?" wondered Small Bear.

He thought and he thought. Then he looked
at a puddle, and he *knew* what to do.

"Small boats need small seas,
so I'll find one!"
decided Small Bear.
He went to the park,
where he found a small sea,
AND…

Small Bear sailed in "Bear's Boat"

by the light of the moon. BUT…

the sea grew too rough! "Bear's Boat" rocked

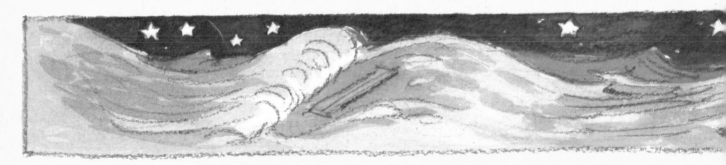

and it rolled and it shattered and SANK!

So he swam and swam until he reached the shore,

where he lay on a rock all shivering and cold.

"Now what shall I do?"
wondered Small Bear.

He thought and he thought.
Then he sighed at the moon,
for he didn't know what to do!
"I'm sick of the sea,
so I think I'll give up!"
decided Small Bear with a sniff.
He curled up by the rock
and went sadly to sleep all alone.

The very next morning a little girl
came and found Small Bear,
and she hugged him
and took him home
and set him to dry by the fire.
"Now what shall I do?"
wondered Small Bear.

He thought and he thought.
Then he looked around the home,
and he *knew* what to do.

"I'm FOUND,
  and I have someone to play with,
  so I'll stay where I am!"
  decided Small Bear,
  and he cuddled up
  close to the girl
  and he stayed . . .

. . . and he never went back to the sea!